THE LEGION
of Lazarus

THE LEGION
of Lazarus
Edmond Hamilton

ÆGYPAN PRESS

From *Imagination,* April 1956.

Special thanks to Greg Weeks, Mary Meehan, and the Online
Distributed Proofreading Team (which can be found at
http://www.pgdp.net).

The Legion of Lazarus
A publication of
ÆGYPAN PRESS

www.aegypan.com

Being expelled from an air lock into deep space was the legal method of execution. But it was also the only way a man could qualify for —
The Legion of Lazarus

It isn't the dying itself. It's what comes before. The waiting, alone in a room without windows, trying to think. The opening of the door, the voices of the men who are going with you but not all the way, the walk down the corridor to the airlock room, the faces of the men, closed and impersonal. They do not enjoy this. Neither do they shrink from it. It's their job.

This is the room. It is small and it has a window. Outside there is no friendly sky, no clouds. There is space, and there is the huge red circle of Mars filling the sky, looking down like an enormous eye upon this tiny moon. But you do not look up. You look out.

There are men out there. They are quite naked. They sleep upon the barren plain, drowsing in a timeless ocean. Their bodies are white as ivory and their hair is loose across their faces. Some of them seem to smile. They lie, and sleep, and the great red eye looks at them forever as they are borne around it.

"It isn't so bad," says one of the men who are with you inside this ultimate room. "Fifty years from now, the rest of us will all be old, or dead."

It is small comfort.

The one garment you have worn is taken from you and the lock door opens, and the fear that cannot possibly become greater does become greater, and then suddenly that terrible crescendo is past. There is no longer any hope, and you learn that without hope there is little to be afraid of. You want now only to get it over with.

You step forward into the lock.

The door behind you shuts. You sense that the one before you is opening, but there is not much time. The burst of air carries you forward. Perhaps you scream, but you are now beyond sound, beyond sight, beyond everything. You do not even feel that it is cold.

I

*T*here is a time for sleep, and a time for waking. But Hyrst had slept heavily, and the waking was hard. He had slept long, and the waking was slow. *Fifty years,* said the dim voice of remembrance. But another part of his mind said, No, it is only tomorrow morning.

Another part of his mind. That was strange. There seemed to be more parts to his mind than he remembered having had before, but they were all confused and hidden behind a veil of mist. Perhaps they were not really there at all. Perhaps —

Fifty years. I have been dead, he thought, *and now I live again. Half a century. Strange.*

Hyrst lay on a narrow bed, in a place of subdued light and antiseptic-smelling air. There was no one else in the room. There was no sound.

Fifty years, he thought. *What is it like now, the house where I lived once, the country, the planet? Where are my children, where are my friends, my enemies, the people I loved, the people I hated?*

Where is Elena? Where is my wife?

A whisper out of nowhere, sad, remote. *Your wife is dead and your children are old. Forget them. Forget the friends and the enemies.*

But I can't forget! cried Hyrst silently in the spaces of his own mind. It was only yesterday —

Fifty years, said the whisper. *And you must forget.*

MacDonald, said Hyrst suddenly. *I didn't kill him. I was innocent. I can't forget that.*

Careful, said the whisper. *Watch out.*

I didn't kill MacDonald. Somebody did. Somebody let me pay for it. Who? Was it Landers? Was it Saul? We four were together out there on Titan, when he died.

Careful, Hyrst. *They're coming. Listen to me. You think this is your own mind speaking, question-and-answer. But it isn't.*

Hyrst sprang upright on the narrow bed, his heart pounding, the sweat running cold on his skin. *Who are you? Where are you? How —*

They're here, said the whisper calmly. *Be quiet.*

Two men came into the ward. "I am Dr. Merridew," said the one in the white coverall, smiling at Hyrst with a brisk professional smile. "This is Warden Meister. We didn't mean to startle you. There are a few questions, before we release you —"

Merridew, said the whisper in Hyrst's mind, *is a psychiatrist. Let me handle this.*

Hyrst sat still, his hands lax between his knees, his eyes wide and fixed in astonishment. He heard the psychiatrist's questions, and he heard the answers he gave to them, but he was merely an instrument, with no conscious volition, it was the whisperer in his mind who was answering. Then the warden shuffled some papers he held in his hand and asked questions of his own.

"You underwent the Humane Penalty without admitting your guilt. For the record, now that the penalty has been paid, do you wish to change your final statements?"

The voice in Hyrst's mind, the secret voice, said swiftly to him. *Don't argue with them, don't get angry, or they'll keep you on and on here.*

"But —" thought Hyrst.

I know you're innocent, but they'll never believe it. They'll keep you on for further psychiatric tests. They might get near the truth, Hyrst — the truth about us.

Suddenly Hyrst began to understand, not all and not clearly, something of what had happened to him. The obscuring mists began to lift from the borders of his mind.

"What is the truth," he asked in that inner quiet, "about us?"

You've spent fifty years in the Valley of the Shadow. You're changed, Hyrst. You're not quite human anymore. No one is, who goes through the freeze. But they don't know that.

"Then you too —"

Yes. And I too changed. And that is why our minds can speak, even though I am on Mars and you are on its moon. But they must not know that. So don't argue, don't show emotion!

The warden was waiting. Hyrst said aloud to him, slowly. "I have no statement to make."

The warden did not seem surprised. He went on, "According to your papers here you also denied knowing the location of the Titanite for which MacDonald was presumably murdered. Do you still deny that?"

Hyrst was honestly surprised. "But surely, by now —"

The warden shrugged. "According to this data, it never came to light."

"I never knew," said Hyrst, "where it was."

"Well," said the warden, "I've asked the question and that's as far as my responsibility goes. But there's a visitor who has permission to see you."

*H*e and the doctor went out. Hyrst watched them go. He thought, So I'm not quite human. Not quite human anymore. Does that make me more, or less, than a man?

Both, said the secret voice. *Their minds are still closed to you. Only our minds – we who have changed too – are open.*

"Who are you?" asked Hyrst.

My name is Shearing. Now listen. When you are released, they'll bring you down here to Mars. I'll be waiting for you. I'll help you.

"Why? What do you care about me, or a murder fifty years old?"

I'll tell you why later, said the whisper of Shearing. *But you must follow my guidance. There's danger for you, Hyrst, from the moment you're released! There are those who have been waiting for you.*

"Danger? But –"

The door opened, and Hyrst's visitor came in. He was a man something over sixty but the deep lines in his face made him look older. His face was grey and drawn and twitching, but it became perfectly rigid and white when he came to the foot of the bed and looked at Hyrst. There was rage in his eyes, a rage so old and weary that it brought tears to them.

"You should have stayed dead," he said to Hyrst. "Why couldn't they let you stay dead?"

Hyrst was shocked and startled. "Who are you? And why –"

The other man was not even listening. His eyelids had closed, and when they opened again they looked on naked agony. "It isn't right," he said. "A murderer should die, and stay dead. Not come back."

"I didn't murder MacDonald," Hyrst said, with the beginnings of anger. "And I don't know why you –"

He stopped. The white, aging face, the tear-filled, furious eyes, he did not quite know what there was about them but it was there, like an old remembered face peeping up through a blur of water for a moment, and then withdrawing again.

After a moment, Hyrst said hoarsely, "What's your name?"

"You wouldn't know it," said the other. "I changed it, long ago."

Hyrst felt a cold, and it seemed that he could not breathe. He said, "But you were only eleven —"

He could not go on. There was a terrible silence between them. He must break it, he could not let it go on. He must speak. But all he could say was to whisper, "I'm not a murderer. You must believe it. I'm going to prove it —"

"You murdered MacDonald. And you murdered my mother. I watched her age and die, spending every penny, spending every drop of her blood and ours, to get you back again. I pretended for fifty years that I too believed you were innocent, when all the time I knew."

Hyrst said, "I'm innocent." He tried to say a name, too, but he could not speak the word.

"No. You're lying, as you lied then. We found out. Mother hired detectives, experts. Over and over, for decades — and always they found the same thing. Landers and Saul could not possibly have killed Mac-Donald, and you were the only other human being there. Proof? I can show you barrels of it. And all of it proof that my father was a murderer."

He leaned a little toward Hyrst, and the tears ran down his lined, careworn face. He said, "All right, you've come back. Alive, still young. But I'm warning you. If you try again to get that Titanite, if you shame us all again after all this time, if you even come near us, I'll kill you."

He went out. Hyrst sat, looking after him, and he thought that no man before him had ever felt what tore him now.

Inside his mind came Shearing's whisper, with a totally unexpected note of compassion. *But some of us have, Hyrst. Welcome to the brotherhood. Welcome to the Legion of Lazarus.*

II

Mars roared and glittered tonight. And how was a man to stand the faces and lights and sounds, when he had come back from the silence of eternity?

Hyrst walked through the flaring streets of Syrtis City with slow and dragging steps. It was like being back on Earth. For this city was not really part of the old dead planet, of the dark barrens that rolled away beneath the night. This was the place of the rocket-men, the miners, the schemers, the workers, who had come from another, younger world. Their bars and entertainment houses flung a sunlike brilliance. Their ships, lifting majestically skyward from the distant spaceport, wrote their flaming sign on the sky. Only here and there moved one of the hooded, robed humanoids who had once owned this world.

The next corner, said the whisper in Hyrst's mind. *Turn there. No, not toward the spaceport. The other way.*

Hyrst thought suddenly, "Shearing."

Yes?

"I am being followed."

His physical ears heard nothing but the voices and music. His physical eyes saw only the street crowd. Yet he knew. He knew it by a picture that kept coming into his mind, of a blurred shape moving always behind him.

Of course you're being followed, came Shearing's thought. *I told you they've been waiting for you. This is the corner. Turn.*

Hyrst turned. It was a darker street, running away from the lights through black warehouses and on the labyrinthine monolithic houses of the humanoids.

Now look back, Shearing commanded. *No, not with your eyes! With your mind. Learn to use your talents.*

Hyrst tried. The blurred image in his mind came clearer, and clearer still, and it was a young man with a vicious mouth and flat uncaring eyes. Hyrst shivered. "Who is he?"

He works for the men who have been waiting for you, Hyrst. Bring him this way.

"This — way?"

Look ahead. With your mind. Can't you learn?

Stung to sudden anger, Hyrst flung out a mental probe with a power he hadn't known he possessed. In a place of total darkness between two warehouses ahead, he saw a tall man lounging at his ease. Shearing laughed.

Yes, it's me. Just walk past me. Don't hurry.

Hyrst glanced backward, mentally at the man following him through the shadows. He was closer now, and quite silent. His face was tight and secret. Hyrst thought, How do I know this Shearing isn't in it with him, taking me into a place where they can both get at me —

He went past the two warehouses and he did not turn his head but his mind saw Shearing waiting in the darkness. Then there was a soft, shapeless sound, and he turned and saw Shearing bending over a huddled form.

"That was unkind of you," said Shearing, speaking aloud but not loudly.

Hyrst, still shaking, said, "But not exactly strange. I've never seen you before. And I still don't know what this is all about."

Shearing smiled, as he knelt beside the prone, unmoving body. Even here in the shadows, Hyrst could see him with these new eyes of the mind. Shearing was a big man. His hair was grizzled along the sides of his head, and his eyes were dark and very keen. He reached out one hand and turned the head of the prone young man, and they looked at the lax, loose face.

"He's not dead?" said Hyrst.

"Of course not. But it will be a while before he wakes."

"But who is he?"

Shearing stood up. "I never saw him before. But I know who he's working for."

*H*yrst flung a sudden question at Shearing, and almost without thinking he followed it to surprise the answer in Shearing's mind. The question was, *Who are you working for?* And the answer was a woman, a tall and handsome woman with angry eyes, standing against a drift of stars. There was a ship, all lonely on a dark plain, and she was pointing to it, and somehow Hyrst knew that it was vitally important to her, and to Shearing, and perhaps even to himself. But before he could do more than register this fleeting vision on his own consciousness, Shearing's mind slammed shut with exactly the same violent effect as a door slammed in his face. He reeled back, throwing up his arms in a futile but instinctive gesture, and Shearing said angrily,

"You're getting too good. I'll give you a social hint — it's customary to knock before you enter."

Hyrst said, still holding the pieces of his head together, "All right — sorry. So who is she?"

"She's one of us. She wants what we want."

"I want only to find out who murdered MacDonald!"

"You want more than that, Hyrst, though you don't know it yet. But MacDonald's murderer is part of what we're after."

He took Hyrst's arm. "We don't have long. Thanks to my guidance, you slipped them all except this one. But they'll be hounding after our trail very quickly."

They went on along the shadowed street. The glare of the lights died back behind them, and they moved in darkness with only the keen stars to watch them, and the cold, gritty wind blowing in from the barrens, and the dark doorways of the mastabalike monolithic houses of the humanoids staring at them like sightless eyes. Hyrst looked up at the bright, tiny moon that crept amid the stars, and a deep shaking took him as he thought of men lying up there in the deathly sleep, of himself lying there year after year. . . .

"In here," said Shearing. It was one of the frigid, musty tombs that the humanoids called home. It was dark and there was nothing in it at all. "We can't risk a light. We don't need it, anyway."

They sat down. Hyrst said desperately, "Listen, I want to know some things. Exactly what are we doing here?"

Shearing answered deliberately, "We are hiding from those who want you, and we are waiting for a chance to go to our friends."

"Our friends? Your friends, maybe. That woman — I don't know her, and —"

"Now *you* listen, Hyrst. I'll tell you this much about us now. We're Lazarites, like you, with the same powers as you. But all Lazarites are not on *our* side."

Hyrst thought about that. "Then those others who are hunting us —"

"There are Lazarites among them, too. Not many, but a few. You don't know us, you don't know them. Do you want to leave me and go back out and let them have you?"

Hyrst remembered the adderlike face of the young man who had come after him through the shadows. After a long moment he said, "Well. But what are *you* after?"

"The thing that MacDonald was killed for, fifty years ago."

Hyrst said, "The Titanite? They said it hadn't ever been found. But how it could have remained hidden so long —"

"I want you," Shearing said, "to tell me all about how MacDonald died. Everything you can remember."

Hyrst asked eagerly, "You think we can find out who killed him? After all this time? God, if we could — my son —"

"Quiet, Hyrst. Go ahead and tell me. Not in words. Just remember what happened, and I'll get it."

Yet, by sheer lifetime habit, Hyrst could not remember without first putting it into words in his own mind, as they two sat in the cold, whispering darkness.

"There were four of us out there on Titan, you must already know that. And only four —"

*F*our men. And one was named MacDonald, an engineer, a secretive, selfish and enormously greedy man. MacDonald was the man who found a fortune, and kept it secret, and died.

Landers was one. A lean, brown, lively man, an excellent physicist with a friendly manner and no obvious ambitions.

Saul was one, and he was big and blond and quiet, a good drinking companion, a good geologist, a lover of good music. If he had any darker passions, he kept them hidden.

Hyrst was the fourth man, and the only one of the four still living. . . .

He remembered now. He saw the black and bitter crags of Titan stark against the glory of the Rings, and he saw two figures moving across a plain of methane snow, their helmets gleaming in the Saturn-light. Behind them in the plain were the flat, half-buried concrete structures of the little refinery, and all around them were the spidery roads where the big half-tracs dragged their loads of uranium ore from the enchaining mountains.

The two men were quarreling.

"You're angry," MacDonald was saying, "because it was *I* who found it."

"Listen," Hyrst said. "We're sick, all three of us, of hearing you brag about it."

"I'll bet you are," said MacDonald smugly. "The first find of a Titanite pocket for years. The rarest, costliest stuff in the System. If you know the way they've been bidding to buy it from me —"

"I do know," Hyrst said. "You've done nothing for weeks but give forth mysterious hints —"

"And you don't like that," MacDonald said. "Of course you don't! It's no part of our refinery deal, it's mine, I've got it and it's hidden where nobody can find it till I sell it. Naturally, you don't like that."

"All *right,*" said Hyrst. "So the Titanite find is all yours. You're still a partner in the refinery, remember. And you've still got an obligation to the rest of us, so you can damn well get in and do your job."

"Don't worry. I've always done my job."

"More or less," said Hyrst. "For your information, I've seen better engineers in grade-school. There's Number Three hoist. It's been busted for a week. Now let's get in there and fix it."

The two figures in Hyrst's memory toiled on, out of the area of roads to the edge of the landing field, where the ships come to take away the refined uranium. Number Three hoist rose in a stiff, ugly column from the ground. It was supposed to fetch the uranium up from the underground storage bins and load it into a specially-built hot-tank ship in position at the dock. But Number Three had balked and refused to perform its task. In this completely automated plant, men were only important when something went wrong. Now something was wrong, and it was up to MacDonald, the mechanical engineer, and Hyrst, the electronics man, to set it right.

Hyrst opened the hatch, and they climbed the metal stairs to the upper chamber. Number Three's brain was here, its scanners, its tabulating and recording apparatus, its signal system. A red light pulsated on a panel, alone in a string of white ones.

"Trouble's in the hoist-mechanism," said Hyrst. "That's your department." He smiled and sat down on a metal bench in the center of the room, with his back to the stair. "D Level."

MacDonald grumbled, and went to a skeletal cage built over a round segment of the floor. Various tools were clipped to the ribs of the cage. MacDonald pulled an extra rayproof protectall over his vac-suit and stepped inside the cage, pressing a button. The cage dropped, into a circular shaft that paralleled the hoist right down to the feeder mechanism.

Hyrst waited. Inside his helmet he could hear Mac-Donald breathing and grumbling as he worked away, repairing a break in the belt. He did not hear anything else. Then something happened, so swiftly that he had never had any memory of it, and some time later he came to and looked for MacDonald. The cage was way down at the bottom of the shaft and MacDonald was in it, with a very massive pedestal-block on top of him. The block had been unbolted from the floor and dragged to the edge of the shaft, and it could not possibly have been an accident that it tumbled in, between the wide-apart ribs of the cage.

And that's how MacDonald died, Hyrst thought — and so *I* died. They said I forced the secret of his Titanite find out of him, and then killed him.

Shearing asked swiftly, "MacDonald never gave you any hint of where he'd hidden the Titanite?"

"No," said Hyrst. He paused, and then said, "It's the Titanite you're after?"

Shearing answered carefully. "In a way, yes. But *we* didn't kill MacDonald for it. Those who did kill him are the men who are after you now. They're afraid you might lead us to the stuff."

Hyrst swore, shaking with sudden anger. "Damn it, I won't be treated like a child. Not by you, by anyone. I want —"

"You want the men who killed MacDonald," said Shearing. "I know. I remember what was in your mind when you met your son."

A weakness took Hyrst and he leaned his forehead against the cold stone wall.

"I'm sorry," said Shearing. "But we want what you want — and more. So much more that you can't dream it. You must trust us."

"Us? That woman?"

Once again in Shearing's mind Hyrst saw the woman with her head against the stars, and the ship looming darkly. He saw the woman much more clearly, and she was like a fire, burning with anger, burning with a single-minded, dedicated purpose. She was beautiful, and frightening.

"She, and others," said Shearing. "Listen. We must go soon. We're to be picked up, secretly. Will you trust us — or would you rather trust yourself to those who are hunting you?"

Hyrst was silent. Shearing said, "Well?"

"I'll go with you," said Hyrst.

They went out into the cold darkness, and Hyrst heard Shearing say in his mind, "I wouldn't try to run —"

But it wasn't Shearing speaking in his mind now, it was a third man.

"I wouldn't try to run —"

Frantically startled, Hyrst threw out his mental vision and saw the men who stood around them in the darkness, four men, three of them holding the wicked little weapons called bee-guns in their hands. The fourth man came closer, a dark slender man with a face like a fox, high-boned, narrow-eyed, smiling. It came to Hyrst that the three with weapons were only ordinary men, and that it was this fourth man whose mind had spoken.

He was speaking aloud now. "I want you alive, believe me — but there are endless gradations between alive and dead. My men are very accurate."

Shearing's face was suddenly drawn and exhausted. "Don't try anything," he warned Hyrst wearily. "He means it."

The dark man shook his head at Shearing. "This wasn't nice of you. You knew we had a particular interest in Mr. Hyrst." He turned to Hyrst and smiled. His teeth were small and very neat and white. "Did you know that Shearing has been keeping a shield over your mind as well as his? A little too large a task for him. When you jarred his mind open for an instant, it was all we needed to lead us here."

He went on. "Mr. Hyrst, my name is Vernon. We'd like you to come with us."

Vernon nodded to the three accurate men, and the whole little group began to walk in the direction of the spaceport. Shearing seemed almost asleep on his feet now. It was as though he had expended all his energy on a task, and failed at it, and was now quiescent, like an empty well waiting to fill again.

"Where are we going?" Hyrst asked, and Vernon answered:

"To see a gentleman you've never heard of, in a place you've never been." He added, with easy friendliness, "Don't worry, Mr. Hyrst, we have nothing against *you*. You're new to this — ah — state of life. You shouldn't be asked to make decisions or agreements until you know both sides of the question. Mr. Shearing was taking an unfair advantage."

Remembering the dark hard purpose Shearing had let him see in his mind, Hyrst could not readily dispute that. But he put out an exploring probe in the direction of Vernon's mind.

It was shut tight.

They walked on, toward the spaceport gates.

III

*A*ll space was before him, hung with the many-colored lights of the stars, intensely brilliant in the black nothing. It was incredibly splendid, but it was too much like what he had looked at with his cold unseeing eyes for fifty years. He looked down — down being relative to where he was standing in the blister-window — and saw the whole Belt swarming by under him like a drift of fireflies. He quivered inwardly with a chill vertigo, and turned away.

Vernon was talking aloud. He had been talking for some time. He was stretched out on a soft, deep lounge, smoking, pretending to sip from a tall glass.

"So you see, Mr. Hyrst, we can help you a lot. It's not easy for a Lazarite — for one of us — to get a job. I know. People have a — well, a *feeling*. Now Mr. Bellaver —"

"Where is Shearing?" asked Hyrst. He came and stood in the center of the room, with the soft lights in his eyes and the soft carpets under his feet. His mind reached out, uneasy and restless, but it seemed to be surrounded by a zone of fog that tangled and confused and deflected it. He could not find Shearing.

"We've been here for hours," he said. "Where is he?"

"Probably talking a deal with Mr. Bellaver. I wouldn't worry. As I was saying, Bellaver Incorporated is interested in men like you. We're the largest builders of spacecraft in the System, and we can afford —"

"I know all about it," said Hyrst impatiently. "Old Quentin Bellaver was busy swallowing up his rivals when I went through the door."

"Then," said Vernon imperturbably, "you should realize how much we can do for you. Electronics is a vital branch —"

Hyrst moved erratically around the room, looking at things and not really seeing them, hearing Vernon's voice but not understanding what it said. He was growing more and more uneasy. It was as though someone was calling to him, urgently, but just out of earshot. He kept straining, with his ears and his mind, and Vernon's voice babbled on, and the barrier was like a wall around his thoughts.

They had been aboard this ship for a long time now, and he had not seen Shearing since they came through the hatch. It was not really a ship, of course. It had no power of its own, depending on powerful tugs to tow it. It was Walter Bellaver's floating pleasure-palace, and the damnedest thing Hyrst had ever seen. Vernon said it could and often did accommodate three or four hundred guests in the utmost luxury. There was nobody aboard it now but Bellaver, Vernon, Hyrst and Shearing, the three very accurate men, and perhaps a dozen others including stewards and the crews of the tugs and Bellaver's yacht. It was named the *Happy Dream*, and it was presently drifting in an excessively lonely orbit high above the ecliptic, between nothing and nowhere.

Vernon had been with him almost constantly. He was getting tired of Vernon. Vernon talked too much.

"Listen," he said. "You can stop selling Bellaver. I'm not looking for a job. Where's Shearing?"

"Oh, forget Shearing," said Vernon, impatient in his turn. "You never heard of him until a few days ago."

"He helped me."

"For reasons of his own."

"What's *your* reason? And Bellaver's?"

"Mr. Bellaver is interested in all social problems. And I'm a Lazarite myself, so naturally I have a sympathy for others like me." Vernon sat up, putting his glass aside on a low table. He had drunk hardly any of the contents.

"Shearing," he said, "is a member of a gang who some time ago stole a particular property of Bellaver Incorporated. You're not involved in the quarrel, Mr. Hyrst. I'd advise you, as a friend, to stay not involved."

Hyrst's mind and his ears were stretched and quivering, straining to hear a cry for help just a little too far away.

"What kind of a property?" asked Hyrst.

Vernon shrugged. "The Bellavers have never said what kind, for fairly obvious reasons."

"Something to do with ships?"

"I suppose so. It isn't important to me. Nor to you, Mr. Hyrst."

"Will you pour me a drink?" said Hyrst, pointing to the cellaret close beside Vernon. "Yes, that's fine. How long ago?"

"What?" asked Vernon, measuring whisky into a glass.

"The theft," said Hyrst, and threw his mind suddenly against the barrier. For one fleeting second he forced a crack in it. "Something over fifty —," said Vernon, and let the glass fall. He spun around from the cellaret and was halfway to his feet when Hyrst hit him. He hit him three or four times before he would stay down, and three or four more before he would lie quiet. Hyrst straightened up, breathing hard. His lip was bleeding and he wiped it with the back of his hand. "That was a little too big a job for *you*, Mr. Vernon," he said viciously. "Trying to keep my mind blanked and under control for hours." He stuffed a handkerchief into Vernon's mouth, and tied him up with his own cummerbund, and shoved him out of sight behind an enormous bed. Then he opened the door carefully, and went out.

*T*here was nobody in the corridor. This was wide and ornate, with doors opening off it, and nothing to show what was behind them or which way to go. Hyrst stood still a minute, getting control of himself. The barrier no longer obscured his mind. He let it rove, finding that every time he did that it was easier, and the images clearer. He heard Shearing again, as he had heard him in that one second when Vernon's guard had faltered. His face became set and ugly. He began to move toward the stern of the *Happy Dream*.

Heavy metal-cloth curtains closed this end of the corridor. Beyond them was a ballroom in which only one dim light now burned, a vastness of black polished floors and crystal windows looking upon space. Hyrst's footsteps were hushed and swallowed up in whispering echoes. He made his way across to another set of curtains, edged between them with infinite caution, and found himself in the upper aisle of an amphitheater.

It was pitch dark where he was, and he stood perfectly still, exploring with his mind. He could not see any guards. The rows of empty seats were arranged in circles around a central pit, large enough for any entertainment Mr. Bellaver might decide to give. The pit was brilliantly lighted, and from somewhere lower down came the intermittent sound of voices.

Also from the pit came Shearing's cries. Hyrst began to tremble with outrage and anger, and his still-uncertain mental control faltered dangerously. Then from out of nowhere, a voice spoke in his mind, and he saw the face of the woman he had seen twice before, the woman Shearing served.

"Careful," she said. "There is a Lazarite with Bellaver. His attention is all on Shearing, but you must keep your mind shielded. I'll help you."

Hyrst whispered. "Thanks." He felt calm now, alert and capable. He crept along the dark aisle, toward the pit.

Mr. Bellaver's theater lacked nothing. The large circular stage area was fitted with upper and lower electro-magnets for the use of acrobats and dancers with null-grav specialties. They could perform without disturbing the regular grav-field of the *Happy Dream*, thus keeping the guests comfortable, and by skillful manipulation of the magnetic fields more spectacular stunts were possible than in ordinary no-gravity.

Shearing was in the pit, between the upper and lower magnets. He wore an acrobat's metal attraction-harness, strapped on over his clothes. When Hyrst looked over the rail he was hanging at the central point of weightlessness, where everything in a man floats free and his senses are lost in a dreadful vertigo unless he has been conditioned over a long period of time to get used to it. Shearing had not been conditioned.

"Careful," said the woman's warning voice in his mind. "His life depends on you. No, don't try to make contact with him! The Lazarite would sense you —"

Shearing began a slow ascension toward the upper magnet as the current was increased, from some unseen

control board. He moved convulsively turning hori-
zontally around the axis of his own middle like a toy
spun on a string. His back was uppermost, and Hyrst
could not see his face.

"Bellaver and the Lazarite," said the woman quietly,
"are trying to learn from Shearing where our ship is.
He has been able so far to keep his mind shielded. He
is — a very brave man. But you'll have to hurry. He's
near the breaking point."

Shearing was now almost level with Hyrst, sus-
pended over that open pit, looking down, a long way.

"You'll have to be quick, Hyrst. Please. Please get him
out of there before we have to kill him."

The current in the magnet was cut and Shearing fell,
with a long neighing scream.

*H*yrst looked down. The repelling force of the lower
magnet cushioned the fall, and the upper magnet took
hold, hard. Shearing stopped about three feet above
the stage floor and started slowly to rise again. He
seemed to be crying. Hyrst turned and ran back to the
top of the aisle. Halfway around the circle he found
steps and went tearing down them. On the next level
— there were three — he saw two men leaning over the
broad rail, watching Shearing.

"Yes, there they are. You must find a weapon —"

Hyrst looked around, blinking like a mole in the
dark. Seats, nothing but seats. Ornamentation, but all
solid. Small metal cylinder, set in a wall niche. Chemi-
cal extinguisher. Yes. Compact and heavy. He took it.

"Hurry. He's almost through —"

The two men were tense and hungry, eager as wolves.
One was the Lazarite, a grey man, old and seamed with
living and none of it good. The other was Bellaver, and

he was young. He was tall and fresh-faced, impeccably shaven, impeccably dressed, the keen, clean, public-spirited executive.

"I can give you more if you want it, Shearing," Bellaver said, his fingers ready on a control-plate set into the broad rail. "How about it?"

"Shut up, Bellaver," whispered the Lazarite aloud. "I've almost got it. Almost —" His face was agonized with concentration.

"Now!"

The woman's voiceless cry in his mind sent Hyrst forward. His hand swung up and then down in a crashing arc, elongated by the heavy cylinder. The Lazarite fell without a sound. He fell across Bellaver, pushing him back from the control-plate, and lay over his feet, bleeding gently into the thick pile of the carpet. Bellaver's mouth and eyes opened wide. He looked at the Lazarite and then at Hyrst. He leaped backward, away from the encumbrance at his ankles, making the first hoarse effort at a shout for help. Hyrst did not give him time to finish it. The first row of seats caught Bellaver and threw him, and Hyrst swung the cylinder again. Bellaver collapsed.

"Was I in time?" Hyrst asked of the woman, in his mind. He thought she was crying when she answered, "Yes." He smiled. He stepped over the Lazarite and went to the control-plate and began to work with it until he had Shearing safely on the floor of the stage. Then he cut the power and ran down another flight of steps to the bottom level. His mind was able to range free now. He could not sense anyone close at hand. Bellaver seemed to have sent underlings elsewhere in the *Happy Dream* while he worked on Shearing. It was nothing for which a man would seek witnesses. Hyrst vaulted the rail onto the stage and dragged Shearing away from the magnet. He felt uncomfortable in all that glare of light. He hauled and grunted until he got Shearing over the rail into the dark. Then he wrestled the harness off him. Shearing sobbed feebly, and retched.

"Can you stand up?" said Hyrst. "Hey. Shearing." He shook him, hard. "Stand up."

He got Shearing up, a one-hundred-and-ninety pound rag doll draped over his shoulders. He began to walk him out of the theater. "Are you still there?" he asked of the woman.

The answer came into his mind swiftly. "Yes. I'll help you watch. Do you see where the skiff is?"

It was in a pod under the belly of the *Happy Dream*. "I see it," said Hyrst.

"Take that. Bellaver's yacht is faster, but you'd need the crew. The skiff you can handle yourself."

*H*e walked Shearing into a fore-and-aft corridor. Shearing's feet were beginning to move of their own accord, and he had stopped retching. But his eyes were still blank and he staggered aimlessly. Hyrst's nerves were prickling with a mixture of fierce satisfaction and fear. Far above in the lush suite he felt Vernon stir and come to. There were men somewhere closer, quite close. He forced his mind to see. Two of the very accurate men who had been with Vernon were playing cards with two others who were apparently stewards. The third one lolled in a chair, smoking. All five were in a lounge just around the corner of a transverse corridor. The door was open.

Without realizing that he had done so, Hyrst took control of Shearing's mind. "Steady, now. We're going past that corner without a sound. You hear me, Shearing? Not a sound."

Shearing's eyes flickered vaguely. He frowned, and his step became steadier. The floor of the corridor was covered in a tough resilient plastic that deadened footsteps. They passed the corner. The men continued to play cards. Hyrst sent up a derisive insult to Vernon and told Shearing to hurry a little. The stair leading down into the pod was just ahead, ten yards, five —

A man appeared in the corridor ahead, coming from some storeroom with a rack of plastic bottles in his hand.

"You'll have to run now," came the woman's thought, coolly. "Don't panic. You can still make it."

The man with the bottles yelled. He began to run toward Hyrst and Shearing, dropping the rack to leave his hands free. In the loungeroom behind them the card-party broke up. Hyrst took Shearing by the arm and clamped down even tighter on his mind, giving him a single command. They ran together, fast.

The men from the lounge poured out into the main corridor. Their voices were confused and very loud. Ahead, the man who had been bringing the bottles was now between Hyrst and the stair. He was a brown, hard man who looked like a pilot. He said, "You better stop," and then he grappled with Hyrst and Shearing. The three of them spun around in a clumsy dance, Shearing moving like an automaton. Hyrst and the pilot flailing away with their fists, and then the pilot fell back hard on the seat of his pants, with the blood bursting out of his nose and his eyes glazing. Hyrst raced for the stair, propelling Shearing. They tumbled down it with a shot from a bee-gun buzzing over their heads. It was a short stair with a double-hatch door at the bottom. They fell through it, and Hyrst slammed it shut almost on the toes of a man coming down the stair behind them. The automatic lock took hold. Hyrst told Shearing, "You can stop now."

A few minutes later, from the great swag belly of the *Happy Dream,* a small space-skiff shot away and was quickly lost in the star-shot immensity above the Belt.

IV

It did not stay lost for long. Shearing was at the controls. The chronometer showed fourteen hours and twenty-seven minutes since they left the *Happy Dream.* Shearing had spent eight of those hours in a species of comatose slumber, from which he had roused out practically normal. Now Hyrst was heavily asleep in the pneumo-chair beside him.

Shearing punched him. "Wake up."

After several more punches Hyrst groaned and opened his eyes. He mumbled a question, and Shearing pointed out the wide curved port that gave full vision forward and on both sides.

"It was a good try," he said, "but I don't think we're going to make it. Look there. No, farther back. See it? Now the other side. And there's one astern."

Still sleepy, but alarmed, Hyrst swung his mental vision around. It was easier than looking. Two fast, powerful tugs from the *Happy Dream,* and Bellaver's yacht. He frowned in heavy concentration. "Bellaver's aboard. He's got a mighty goose-egg on his head. Vernon too, with his shields up tight. The three accurate men and the pilot — his nose is a thing of beauty

— plus crew. Nine in all. Two men each to the tugs. The other Lazarite, the one I laid out — he's not along."

Shearing nodded approvingly. "You're getting good. Now take a glance at our fuel-tanks and tell me what you see."

Hyrst sat up straight, fully awake. "Practically," he said, "nothing."

"This skiff was meant for short hops only. We've got enough for perhaps another forty-five minutes, less if we get too involved. They're faster than we are, so they'll catch up to us — oh, say in about half an hour. We have friends coming —"

"Friends?"

"Certainly. You don't think we let each other down, do you? Not the brotherhood. But they had to come from a long way off. We can't possibly rendezvous under an hour and a half, maybe more if —"

"I know," said Hyrst. "If we all get involved." He looked out the port. In the beginning, following directions from the young woman — whose name he had never thought to ask — he had set a course that plunged him deep into one of the wildest sectors of the Belt. He was not a pilot. He could, like most men of his time, handle a simple craft under simple conditions, but these conditions were not simple. The skiff's radar was short-range and it had no automatic deflection reflexes. Hyrst had had to fly on ESP, spotting meteor swarms, asteroids, debris of all sorts in this poetically named hell-hole, the Path of Minor Worlds, and then figuring out how to get by, through, or over them without a crash. Shearing had relieved him just in time.

He glowered at the whirling, glittering mess outside, the dust, the shards and fragments of a shattered world. It merged into mist and his mind was roving again. Shearing jockeyed the controls. He was flying esper too. The tugs and Bellaver's fast yacht were closing up the gap. The level in the tanks went down, used up not in free fall but in the constant maneuvering.

Hyrst swung mentally inboard to check vac-suits and equipment in the locker, and then out again. His vision was strong and free. He could look at the Sun, and see the splendid fires of the corona. He could look at Mars, old and cold and dried-up, and at Jupiter, massive and sullen and totally useless except as an anchor for its family of crazy moons. He could look farther than that. He could look at the stars. In a little while, he thought, he could look at whole galaxies. His heart pounded and the breath came hot and hard into his lungs. It was a good feeling. It made all that had gone before almost worthwhile. The primal immensities drew him, the black gulfs lit with gold and crimson and peacock-colored flames. He wanted to go farther and farther, into —

"You're learning too fast," said Shearing dryly. "Stick to something small and close and sordid, namely an asteroid where we can land."

"I found one," said Hyrst. "There."

Shearing followed his mental nudge. "Hell," he said, "couldn't you have spotted something better? These Valhallas give me the creeps."

"The others within reach are too small, or there's no cover. We'll have quite a little time to wait. I take it you would like to be alive when your friends come."

Vernon's thought broke in on them abruptly. "You have just one chance of that, and that's to give yourselves up, right now."

"Does the socially-conscious Mr. Bellaver still want to give me that job?" asked Hyrst.

"I'm warning you," said Vernon.

"Your mind is full of hate," said Hyrst. "Cleanse it." He shut Vernon out as easily as hanging up a phone. Under stress, his new powers were developing rapidly. He felt a little drunk with them. Shearing said, "Don't get above yourself, boy. You're still a cub, you know." Then he grinned briefly and added, "By the way, thanks."

Hyrst said, "I owed it to you. And you can thank your lady friend, too. She had a big hand in it."

"Christina," said Shearing softly. "Yes."

He dropped the skiff sharply in a descending curve, toward the asteroid.

"Do you think," said Hyrst, "you could now tell me what the devil this is all about?"

Shearing said, "We've got a starship."

Hyrst stared. For a long time he didn't say anything. Then, "You've got a starship? But nobody has! People talk of someday reaching other stars, but nobody tried yet, nobody *could* try —" He broke off, suddenly remembering a dark, lonely ship, and a woman with angry eyes watching it. Even in his astonishment, things began to come clearer to him. "So that's it — a starship. And Bellaver wants it?"

Shearing nodded.

"Well," said Hyrst. "Go on."

"You've already developed some amazing mental capabilities since you came back from beyond the door. You'll find that's only the beginning. The radiation, the exposure — something. The simple act of pseudo-death, perhaps. Anyway, the brain is altered, stepped up, a great deal of its normally unused potential released. You've always been a fair-to-middling technician. You'll find your rating boosted, eventually, to the genius level."

The skiff veered wildly as Shearing dodged a whizzing chunk of rock the size of a skyscraper.

"That's one reason," he said, "why we wanted to get you before Bellaver did. The number of technicians undergoing the Humane Penalty is quite small. We — the brotherhood — need all of them we can get."

"But that wasn't the main reason you wanted me?" pressed Hyrst.

Shearing looked at him. "No. We wanted you mainly because you were present when MacDonald died. Handled right —"

He paused. The asteroid was rushing at them, and Bellaver's ships were close behind. Hyrst was already in a vac-suit, all but the helmet.

"Take the controls," said Shearing. "As she goes. Don't worry, I'll make the landing." He pulled the vac-suit on. "Handled right," he said, "you might be the key to that murder, and to the mystery behind it that the brotherhood *must* solve."

He took the controls again. They helped each other on with their helmets. The asteroid filled the port, a wild, weird jumble of vari-colored rock.

"I don't see how," said Hyrst, into his helmet mike.

"Latent impressions," answered Shearing briefly, and sent the skiff skittering in between two great black monoliths, to settle with a jar on a pan of rock as smooth and naked as a ballroom floor.

"Make it fast," said Shearing. "They're right on top of us."

*T*he skiff, designed as Sheering had said for short hops, could not accommodate the extra weight and bulk of an airlock. You were supposed to land in atmosphere. If you didn't, you just pushed a release-button and hung on. The air was exhausted in one whistling swoosh that took with it everything loose.

The moisture in it crystallized instantly, and before this frozen drift had even begun to settle, Hyrst and Shearing were on their way.

They crossed the rock pan in great swaggering bounds. The gravity was light, the horizon only twenty or so miles away. Literally in his mind's eye Hyrst could see the three ships arrowing at them. He opened contact with Vernon, knowing Shearing had done so too. Vernon had been looking for them.

"Mr. Bellaver still prefers to have you alive," he said. "If you'll wait quietly beside the skiff, we'll take you aboard."

Shearing gave him a hard answer.

"Very well," said Vernon. "Mr. Bellaver wants me to make it clear to you that he doesn't intend for you to get away. So you can interpret that as you please. Be seeing you."

He broke contact, knowing that Hyrst and Shearing would close him out. From now on, Hyrst realized, he would keep track of them the way he and Shearing had kept track of obstructions in the path of flight, by mental "sight." The yacht was extremely close. Suddenly Hyrst had a confused glimpse of a hand on a control-lever overlapped by a view of the black-mouthed tubes of the yacht's belly-jets. He dived, literally, into a crack between one of the monoliths and a slab that leaned against its base, dragging Shearing with him.

The yacht swept over. Nothing happened. It dropped out of sight, braking for a landing.

"Imagination," said Shearing. "You realize a possibility, and you think it's so. Tricky. But I don't blame you. The safe side is the best one."

Hyrst looked out the crack. One of the tugs was coming in to land beside the skiff, while the other one circled.

"Now what?" he said. "I suppose we can dodge them for a while, but we can't hide from Vernon."

Shearing chuckled. He had got his look of tough competence back. He seemed almost to be enjoying himself. "I told you you were only a cub. How do you suppose we've kept the starship hidden all these years? Watch."

In the flick of a second Hyrst went blind and deaf. Then he realized that it was only his mental eyes and ears that were blanked out as though a curtain had been drawn across them. His physical eyes were still clear and sharp, and when Shearing's voice came over the helmet audio he heard it without trouble.

"This is called the cloak. I suppose you could call it an extension of the shield, though it's more like a force field. It's no bar to physical vision, and it has the one great disadvantage of being opaque both ways to mental energy. But it does act as a deflector. If Vernon follows us now, he'll have to do it the hard way. Stick close by me, so I don't have too wide a spread. And it'll be up to you to lead. I can't do both. Let's go."

Hyrst had, unconsciously, become so used to his new perceptions that it made him feel dull and helpless to be without them. He led off down one of the smooth rock avenues, going away from the skiff and the tug which had just landed.

On either side of the avenue were monoliths, irregularly spaced and of different sizes and heights but following an apparently orderly plan. The light of the distant sun lay raw and blinding on them, casting shadows as black and sharp-edged as though drawn upon the rock with india ink.

You could see faces in the monoliths. You could see mighty outlines, singly and in groups, of gods and beasts and men, in combat, in suppliance, in death and burial. That was why these asteroids were called Valhallas. Twenty-six of them had been found so far, and studied, and still no one could say certainly whether or not the hands of any living beings had fashioned them. They might be actual monuments, defaced by cosmic dust, by collision with the myriad fragments of the Belt, by time. They might be one of Nature's casual jokes, created by the same agencies. No actual tombs had been found, nor tools, nor definitely identifiable artifacts. But still the feeling persisted, in the airless silence of the avenues, that some passing race had paused and wrought for itself a memorial more enduring than its fame, and then gone on into the great galactic sea, never to return.

*H*yrst had never been on a Valhalla before. He understood why Shearing had not wanted to land and he wished now that they hadn't. There was something overwhelmingly sad and awesome about these leaning, towering figures of stone, moving forever in their lonely orbit, going nowhere, returning to nowhere.

Then he saw the second tug overhead. He forgot his daydreams. "They're going to act as a spotter," he said. Shearing grunted but did not speak. His whole mind was concentrated on maintaining the cloak. Hyrst stopped him still in the pitchy shadow under what might have been a kneeling woman sixty feet high. He watched the tug. It lazed away, circling slowly, and he did not think it had seen them. He could not any longer see the place where they had landed, but he assumed that by now the yacht had looped back and come in — if not there somewhere close by. They could figure on nine to eleven men hunting them, depending on whether they left the ships guarded or not. Either way, it was too many.

"Listen," he said aloud to Shearing. "Listen, I want to ask you. What you said about latent impressions — you think I might have seen and heard the killer even though I was unconscious?"

"Especially heard. Possible. With your increased power, and ours, impressions received through sense-channels but not recognized at the time or remembered later might be recovered." He shook his head. "Don't bother me."

"I just wanted to know," said Hyrst. He thought of his son, and the two daughters he hoped he would never see. He thought of Elena. It was too late to do anything for her, but the others were still living. So was he, and he intended to stay that way, at least until he had done what he set out to do.

"Old Bellaver was behind that killing, wasn't he? Old Quentin, this one's grandfather."

"Yes. Don't bother me."

"One thing more. Do we Lazarites live longer than men?"

Shearing gave him a curious, brief look. "Yes."

The tug was out of sight behind a massive rearing shape that seemed to clutch a broken ship between its paws. Symbolic, perhaps, of space? Who knew? Hyrst led Shearing in wild impalalike leaps across an open space, and into a narrow way that twisted, filled with darkness, among the bases of a group that resembled an outlandish procession following a king.

"How much longer?"

"Humane Penalty first came in a hundred and four-teen years ago, right? After Seitz' method was perfected for saving spacemen. I was one of the first they used it on."

"My God," said Hyrst. Yet, somehow, he was not as surprised as he might have been.

"I've aged," said Shearing apologetically. "I was only twenty-seven then."

They crouched, beside a humped shape like a gigantic lizard with a long tail. The tug swung overhead and slowly on.

Hyrst said, "Then it's possible the one who killed MacDonald is still alive?"

"Possible. Probable."

Hyrst bared his teeth, in what was not at all like a smile. "Good," he said. "That makes me happy."

They did not do any talking after that. They had had their helmet radios operating on practically no power at all, so that they couldn't be picked up outside a radius of a few yards, but even that might be too close, now that Bellaver's men had had time to get suited and fan out. They shut them off entirely, communicating by yanks and nudges.

*F*or what seemed to Hyrst like a very long time, but which was probably less than half an hour in measured minutes, they dodged from one patch of shadow to another, following an erratic course that Hyrst thought would lead them away from the ships. Once more the tug went over, slow, and then Hyrst didn't see it again. The idea that they might have given up occurred to him but he dismissed it as absurd. With the helmet mike shut off, the silence was beginning to get on his nerves. Once he looked up and saw a piece of cosmic debris smash into a monolith. Dust and splinters flew, and a great fragment broke off and fell slowly downward, bumping and rebounding, and all of it as soundless as a dream. You couldn't hear yourself walk, you couldn't hear anything but the roar of your own breathing and the pounding of your own blood. The grotesque rocky avenues could hide an army, stealthy, creeping —

There was a hill, or at least a higher eminence, crowned with what might have been the cyclopean image of a man stretched out on a noble catafalque, with hooded giants standing by in attitudes of mourning. It seemed like the best place to stop that Hyrst had seen, with plenty of cover and a view of the surrounding area. With luck, you might stay hidden there a long time. He jogged Shearing's elbow and pointed, and Shearing nodded. There was a wide, almost circular sweep of open rock around the base of the hill. Hyrst looked carefully for the tug. There was no sign of it. He tore out across the open, with Shearing at his heels.

The tug swooped over, going fast this time. It could not possibly have missed them. Shearing dropped the cloak with a grunt. "No use for that anymore," he said. They bounded up the hillside and in among the mourning figures. The tug whipped around in a tight spiral and hung over the hill. Hyrst shook the sweat out of his eyes. His mind was clear again. The tug's skipper was babbling into his communicator, and in another place on the asteroid Hyrst could mentally see a thin skirmish line spread out, and in still another four men in a bunch. They all picked up and began to move, toward the hill.

Shearing said, nodding spaceward, "Our friends are on the way. If we can hold out —"

"Fat chance," said Hyrst. "They're armed, and all we've got is flare-pistols." But he looked around. His eyes detected nothing but rock, hard sunlight, and deep shadow, but his mind saw that one of the black blots at the base of the main block, the catafalque, was more than a shadow. He slid into a crack that resembled a passage, being rounded rather than ragged. Shearing was right behind him. "I don't like this," he said, "but I suppose there's no help for it."

The crack led down into a cave, or chamber, too irregularly shaped to be artificial, too smoothly surfaced and floored to be natural. There was nothing in it but a block of stone, nine feet or so long and about four feet wide by five feet high. It seemed to be a natural part of the floor, but Hyrst avoided it. On the opposite, the sunward side, there was a small windowlike aperture that admitted a ray of blinding radiance, sharply defined and doing nothing to illumine the dark on either side of it.

Vernon's thought came to them, hard, triumphant, peremptory. "Mr. Bellaver says you have ten minutes to come out. After that, no mercy."

V

*T*he minutes slid past, sections of eternity arbitrarily measured by the standards of another planet and having no relevance at all on this tiny whirling rock. The beam of light from the small aperture moved visibly across the opposite wall. Hyrst watched it, blinking. Outside, Bellaver's men were drawn up in a wide crescent across the hill in front of the catafalque. They waited.

"No mercy," said Hyrst softly. "No mercy, is it?" He bent over and began to loosen the clamps that held the lead weights to the soles of his boots.

"It isn't mercy we need," said Shearing. "It's time."

"How much?"

"Look for yourself."

Hyrst shifted his attention to space. There was a ship in it, heading toward the asteroid, and coming fast. Hyrst frowned, doing in his head without thinking about it a calculation that would have required a computer in his former life.

"Twenty-three minutes and seventeen seconds," he said, "inclusive of the four remaining."

He finished getting the weights off his boots. He handed one to Shearing. Then he half-climbed, half-floated up the wall and settled himself above the entrance, where there was a slight concavity in the rock to give him hold.

"Shearing," he said.

"What?" He was settling himself beside the mouth of the crack, where a man would have to come clear inside to get a shot at him.

"A starship implies the intention to go to the stars. Why haven't you?"

"For the simplest reason in the world," said Shearing bitterly. "The damn thing can't fly."

"But —" said Hyrst, in astonishment.

"It isn't finished. It's been building for over seventy years now, and a long and painful process that's been, too, Hyrst — doing it bit by bit in secret, and every bit having to be dreamed up out of whole cloth, and often discarded and dreamed up again, because the principle of a workable star-drive has never been formulated before. And it still isn't finished. It can't be finished, unless —"

He stopped, and both men turned their attention to the outside.

"Bellaver's looking at his chrono," said Hyrst. "Go ahead, we've got a minute."

Shearing continued, "unless we can get hold of enough Titanite to build the hyper-shift relays. Nothing else has a fast enough reaction time, and the necessary load-capacity. We must have burned out a thousand different test-boards, trying."

"Can't you buy it?" asked Hyrst. The question sounded reasonable, but he knew as he said it that it was a foolish one. "I mean, I know the stuff is scarcer than virtue and worth astronomical sums — that's what MacDonald was so happy about — but —"

"The Bellaver Corporation had a corner on the stuff before our ship was even thought of. That's what brought this whole damned mess about. Some of our people — not saying why they wanted it, of course — tried to buy some from Bellaver in the usual way, and one of them must have been incautious about his shield. Because a Lazarite working for Bellaver caught a mental hint of the starship, and the reason for the Titanite, and that was it. Three generations of Bellavers have been after us for the star-drive, and it's developed into a secret war as bitter as any ever fought on the battlefield. They hold all the Titanite, we hold the ship, and perhaps now you're beginning to see why Mac-Donald was killed, and why you're so important to both sides."

"Beginning to," said Hyrst. "But only beginning."

"MacDonald found a Titanite pocket. And as you know, a Titanite pocket isn't very big. One man can break the crude stuff, fill a sack with it, and tote it on his own back if he doesn't have a power-sled."

"MacDonald had a sled."

"And he used it. He cleaned out his pocket, afraid somebody else would track him to it, and he hid the wretched ore somewhere. Then he began to dicker. He approached the Bellaver Corporation, and we heard of it and approached *him*. He tried playing us off against Bellaver to boost the price, and suddenly he was dead and you were accused of his murder. We thought you really had done it, because no Titanite turned up, and we knew Bellaver hadn't gotten it from him. We'd watched too closely. It wasn't until some years later that one of our people learned that MacDonald had threatened a little too loudly to sell to us unless Bellaver practically tripled his offer — and of course Bellaver didn't dare do that. A price so much out of line even for Titanite would have stirred all the rival shipbuilders to unwelcome curiosity. So, we figured, Bellaver had had him killed."

"But what happened to the Titanite?"

"That," said Shearing, "is what nobody knows. Bellaver must have figured that if his tame Lazarites couldn't find where MacDonald had put it, we couldn't either. He was right. With all our combined mental probes and conventional detectors we haven't been able to track it down. And we haven't been able to find anymore pockets, either. Bellaver Corporation got exclusive mineral rights to the whole damned moon. They even own the refinery now."

Hyrst shook his head. "Latent impressions or not, I don't see how I can help on that. If MacDonald had given the killer any clue —"

A beam of bright blue light no thicker than a pencil struck in through the mouth of the passage. It touched the side of the large stone block. The stone turned molten and ran, and then the beam flicked off, leaving a place that glowed briefly red. Shearing said, "I guess our ten minutes are up."

They were. For a second or two nothing more happened and then Hyrst saw something come sailing in through the crack. His mind told him what it was just barely in time to shut his eyes. There was a flash that dazzled him even through his closed lids, and the flash became a glare that did not lessen. Bellaver's men had tossed in a long-term flare, and almost at once someone followed it, in the hope of catching Hyrst and Shearing blinded and off guard. The eyes of Hyrst's mind, unaffected by light, clearly showed him the suited figure just below him, with its bubble helmet covered by a glare-shield. They directed him with perfect accuracy in the downward sweep of the lead weight he had taken from his boot, and which he still held in his hand. The bubble helmet was very strong, and the gravity very light, but the concussion was enough to drop the man unconscious. Just about thought Hyrst, what happened to me there in the hoist tower, when MacDonald died. Shearing, who had by now adjusted his own glare-shield stooped quickly and took the man's gun.

He said aloud, over the helmet communicator, "The next one that steps through here gets it. Do you hear that, Bellaver?"

Bellaver's voice answered. "Listen, Shearing, I was wrong. I admit it. Let's calm down and start over again. I —"

"Ten minutes ago it was no mercy."

"It's hard for me to behave reasonably about this business. You know what it means to me, what it meant to my father and *his* father. But I'm willing to do anything, Shearing, if you'll make a deal."

"I'll make a deal. Readily. Eagerly. Give back what your grandfather stole from us, and we'll call it square."

"Oh no we won't," said Hyrst grimly, breaking in. "Not until I find who killed MacDonald."

"All right," said Bellaver. "Wilson, break out the grenades."

The entire surface of Hyrst's body burst into a flaring sweat. For one panic-stricken second he wanted to rush out the crack pleading for mercy. Then he got his feet against the wall and pushed hard, and went plunging across the chamber in a sort of floating dive. Shearing got there at the same time and helped to pull him down. They huddled together on the floor, with the coffin-shaped block between them and the crack. Hyrst sent out a frantic mental call to hurry, directed at the spaceship of the brotherhood.

"They're all going to hurry," said Shearing. "Vernon has found the ship now. He's telling Bellaver. Here comes the grenade —"

Small round glittering thing of death, curving light and graceful through the airless gloom. It comes so slowly, and the flesh shrinks quivering upon itself until it is nothing more than a handful of simple fear. Outside the men are running away, and the one who has thrown the grenade from the cramped, constructing vantage of the crack is running after them, and Shearing is crying with his mind Will it to fall short, *will it to fall sh* —

There is a great brilliance, and the rock leaps, but there is not the slightest sound.

VI

"The Ram, the Bull, the Heavenly Twins,
And next the Crab the Lion Shine.
The Virgin and the Scales —"

*T*he old zodiacal rhyme was running through Hyrst's mind, and that was the only thing that was in his mind.

The Virgin and the Scales.

Yes. And she's very beautiful, too, thought Hyrst. But she shouldn't be *holding* the Scales. That's all wrong. The Scales come next, and then the Scorpion — Scorpio — and the Archer — Sagittarius —

And anyway they aren't scales, they're a pair of big golden stars, and she's putting them down, and they're melting together. There's only one of them, and it's not a star at all, really. It's a polished metal jug, reflecting the light, and —

The Virgin smiled. "The doctor said you were coming around. I brought you something to drink."

Reality returned to Hyrst with a rush. "You're Christina," he said, and tried to sit up. He was dizzy, and she helped him, and he said, "I guess it did fall short."

"What?"

"The grenade. The last thing I remember is Shearing — Wait. Where is Shearing?"

"Sitting up in the lounge, nursing his bruises. Yes, it fell short, but I don't think telekinetics had much to do with that. We've never been able to control matter convincingly. There. All right?"

"Fine. How did you get us out?"

"Of course the grenade had made the entrance impassible — we had to cut our way in through the outer wall. We had a clear field. Bellaver's men had all gone back to their ships. They thought you were dead, and to tell you the truth we thought you must be, too. But you didn't quite 'feel' dead, so we dug you out."

"Thanks," said Hyrst. "I suppose they know different now."

He was in a ship's sick-bay. From the erratic crash and shudder of the lateral jets, they were beating their way through the Belt, and at a high rate of speed. Hyrst sent a glance back into space. The tugs and Bellaver's yacht were following, but this time only the yacht had a chance. The tugs were dropping hopelessly behind.

"Yes, they soon found out once we got you out, but with any luck we'll lose them," said Christina. She sat down beside the bunk, where she could see his face. "Shearing told you about the ship."

"The starship. Yes." He looked at her. Suddenly he laughed. "You're not a goddess at all."

"Who said I was?"

"Shearing. Or anyway, his mind. Ten feet tall, and crowned with stars — I was afraid of you." He leaned closer. "Your eyes, though. They are angry."

"So will yours be," she said, "when you've fought the Bellavers as long as we have."

"There are still things I don't understand. Why you built the ship, why you've kept it secret from everyone, not just Bellaver, what you plan to do with it — how *you* came to be one of the Brotherhood."

She smiled. "The Seitz method was originated to save wreck-victims frozen in deep space. Remember? Quite a few of us never went through the door at all, innocent or guilty. But that makes no difference, once you've come back from out there." She put her hand on his. "You've learned fast, but you're only on the threshold. There's no need for words with us. Open your mind —"

*H*e did so. At first it was no different from the contact he had had with Shearing's mind, or with Christina's before on the *Happy Dream.* Thoughts came to him clearly phrased — *You want to know why we built the ship, what we plan to do with it* — and it was only after some time that he realized the words had stopped and he was receiving Christina's emotions, her memories and opinions, her disappointments and her dreams, as simply and directly as though they were his own.

You haven't had time yet, they told him without words, to realize how alone you are. You haven't tried, as most of us do at first, to be human again, to fit yourself into life as though the gap of time was not there, as though nothing had changed. You haven't watched people getting old around you while you have hardly added a grey hair. You haven't had to move from one place to another, one job, one group of friends to another, because sooner or later they sense something wrong about you. You haven't had to hide your new powers as you would hide a disease because people would fear and hate you, perhaps even kill you, if they knew. That's why there is a brotherhood. And that's why we built the ship.

Symbol of flight. Symbol of freedom. A universe wide beyond imagining, thronging with many colored guns, with new worlds where men in a human society could build a society of their own. *No boundaries beyond which the mind cannot dare to go. All space, all time, all knowledge – free!*

Once more he saw those wide dark seas between the suns. His mind raced with hers through the cold-flaming nebulae, wheeled blinded and stunned past the hiving stars of Hercules, looked in eager fascination at the splendid spiral of Andromeda – no longer, perhaps, beyond reach, for what are time and space to the intangible forces of the mind?

Then that wild flight ceased, and instead there was a smaller vision, misty and only half realized, of houses and streets, a place where they could live and be what they were, openly and without fear.

Can you understand now, she asked him, *what they would think if they knew about the ship? Can you understand that they would be afraid to have us colonizing out there, afraid of what we might do?*

He understood. At the very least, if the truth were known, the Lazarites would never be free again. They would be taken and tested and examined and lectured about, legislated over, restricted, governed, and used. They might be fairly paid for their ship and whatever other advancements they might develop, but they would never be permitted to use them.

With sudden savage eagerness Hyrst said, "But first of all I must know who killed MacDonald. Shearing explained about the latent impressions. I'm ready."

She stood up, regarding him with grave eyes. "There's no guarantee it will work. Sometimes it does. Sometimes not."

Hyrst thought about the tired, grey-haired man who had stood at the foot of his bed. "It'll work. It's got to."

He added, "If it doesn't, I'll tear the truth out of Bellaver with my hands."

"It may come to that," she said grimly. "But we'll hope. Lie quiet. I'll make the arrangements."

An hour later Hyrst lay on the padded table in the middle of the sick-bay. The ship spun and whirled and leaped in a sort of insane dance, and Hyrst was strapped to the table to prevent his being thrown off. He had known that the ship was maneuvering in the thickest swarm area of the Belt with four pilots mind-linked and flying esper, trying to out-dare Bellaver. Two others were keeping Vernon blanked, and they hoped that either Bellaver himself or his radar-deflector system would give up. Hyrst had known this, but now he was no longer interested. He was barely conscious of the lurching of the ship. They had given him some sort of a drug, and he lay relaxed and pliant in a pleasant suspension of all worries, looking vaguely up at the faces that were bent over him. Finally he closed his eyes, and even they were gone.

*H*e was crossing the plain of methane snow with MacDonald, under the glowing Rings. At first it was all a little blurred, but gradually the memory cleared until he was aware of each tiny detail far more clearly than he had been at the time — the texture of the material from which MacDonald's suit was made, the infinitesimal shadow underscoring every roughness of the snow, the exact sensation of walking in his leaded boots, the whisper and whistle of his oxygen system. He quarreled again with MacDonald, not missing a word. He climbed with him into the tower of Number Three hoist and examined the signal lights, and sat down on the bench, smiling, to wait.

He sweated inside his suit. He would take a shower when he got back to quarters. He wished for a smoke. MacDonald's steady grumbling and cursing filled his helmet. He listened, enjoying it. Hope you bang yourself with your own clumsy hammer. And I wish you joy of your fortune. If you have as many friends rich as you had poor you won't have any. There was an itch under his left arm. He pressed the suit in with his right and wriggled his body against it. It didn't do any good. Damn suits. Damn Titan. Lucky Elena, back on Earth with the kids. Making good money, though. Won't be long before I can go back and live like a human being. Now his nose itched, and MacDonald was still grumbling. There was the faintest ghost of a sound and then *crack*, then nothing, dark, cold, sinking, very weak, gone. Nothing, nothing. I come to in the cold silence and look down the shaft at MacDonald and he is dead.

Go back a bit. Slow. That's right. Easy. Back to Elena and the kids.

Lucky Elena, in the sun and the warm sweet air. Lucky kids. But I'm lucky too. I can go back to them soon. My nose itches. Why does your nose always itch when you've got a helmet on, or your hands all over grease? Listen to MacDonald, damning the belt, damning the tools, damning everything in sight. Is that a footstep? The air is thin and poisonous, but it carries sound. Somebody coming behind me? Split second, no time to look or think. *Crack.* Cold. Dark. Nothing.

Let's go back again. Don't hurry. We've all the time in the world. Go back to the footsteps you heard behind you.

Almost heard. And then I black and cold. Heavy. Flat. Face heavy against helmet, cold. Lying down. Must get up, must get up, danger. Far away. Can't.

MacDonald is screaming. Let the lift alone, what are you doing, Hyrst? Hyrst! Shut up, you greedy little man, and listen. You're not Hyrst — who are you? That doesn't matter. I know, you're from Bellaver. Bellaver sent you to steal the Titanite. Well, you won't get it. It's where nobody will ever get it unless I show them how. Good. That's good, MacDonald. That's what I wanted to know. You see, *we* don't need the Titanite.

MacDonald screams again and the lift goes down with a roar and a rattle of severed chain.

Heavy footsteps, shaking the floor by my head. Someone turns me over, speaks to me, bending close. Light is grey and strange. I try to rouse. I can't. The man is satisfied. He drops me and goes away, but I have seen his face inside his helmet. I hear him working on some metal thing with a tool. He is whistling a little under his breath. MacDonald is not screaming now. From time to time he whimpers. But I have seen the killer's face.

I have seen his face.

I have seen —

Take it easy, Hyrst. Take your time.

Elena is dead, and this is Christina bending over me.

I have seen the killer's face.

It is the face of Vernon.

VII

*T*here was Christina, and there was Shearing, and there were two more he did not know, leaning over him. The drug was wearing off a little, and Hyrst could see them more clearly, see the bitter disappointment in their eyes.

"Is that all?" Christina said. "Are you sure? Go back again —"

They took him back again, and it was the same.

"That's all MacDonald said? Then we're no closer to the Titanite than we were before."

Hyrst was not interested in the Titanite. "Vernon," he said. Something red and wild rose up in him, and he tried to tear away the straps that held him. "Vernon. I'll get him —"

"Later, Hyrst," said Shearing, and sighed. "Lie still a bit. He's on Bellaver's yacht, remember? Quite out of reach. Now think. MacDonald said, You won't get it, it's where nobody will ever get it —"

"What's the use?" said Christina, turning away. "It was a faint hope anyway. Dying men don't draw obliging maps for you." She sat down on the edge of a bunk and put her head in her hands. "We might as well give up. You know that."

One of the two Lazarites who had done the latent probe on Hyrst said with hollow hopefulness, "Perhaps if we let him rest a while and then go over it again —"

"Let me up out of here," said Hyrst, still groggy with the drug. "I want Vernon."

"I'll help you get him," said Shearing, "if you'll tell me what MacDonald meant when he said *nobody will ever get it unless I show them how.*"

"How the devil do I know?" Hyrst tugged at the straps, raging. "Let me up."

"But you knew MacDonald well. You worked with him and beside him for years."

"Does that tell me where he hid the Titanite? Don't be an ass, Shearing. Let me up."

"But," said Shearing equably, "he didn't say *where.* He said *how.*"

"Isn't that the same thing?"

"Is it? Listen. Nobody will ever get it unless I show them where. Nobody will ever get it unless I show them how."

Hyrst stopped fighting the straps. He began to frown. Christina lifted her head again. She did not say anything. The two Lazarites who had done the probe stood still and held their breath.

Shearing's mind touched Hyrst's stroking it as with soothing fingers. "Let's think about that for a minute. Let your thoughts move freely. MacDonald was an engineer. The engineer. Of the four, he alone knew every inch of the physical set-up of the refinery. So?"

"Yes. That's right. But that doesn't say where — Wait a minute, though. If he'd just shoved it in a crack somewhere in the mountains, he'd know a detector might find it, more easily than before it was dug. He'd have put it some where deep, deeper than he could possibly dig. Maybe in an abandoned mine?"

"No place," said Shearing, "is too deep for us to probe. We've examined every abandoned mine on that side of Titan. And it doesn't fit, anyway. No. Try again."

"He wouldn't have brought it back to the refinery. One of us would be sure to find it. Unless, of course —"

Hyrst stopped, and the tension in the sick-bay tightened another notch. The ship lurched sharply, swerved, and shot upward with a deafening thunder of rocket-blasts. Hyrst shut his eyes, thinking hard.

"Unless he put it in some place so dangerous that nobody ever went there. A place where even he didn't go, but which he would know about being the engineer."

"Can you think of anyplace that would answer that description?"

"Yes," said Hyrst slowly. "The underground storage bins. They're always hot, even when they're empty. Anything hidden near them would be blanketed by radiation. No detector would see anything but uranium. Probably even you wouldn't."

"No," said Shearing, looking amazed. "Probably we wouldn't. The radioactive disturbance would be too strong to get through, even if we were looking for something beyond it, which we weren't."

Christina had sprung up. Now she bent over Hyrst and said, "But is there a way it could have been done? Obviously, the Titanite couldn't have been put directly into the bin with the uranium — if nothing else, it would have been shipped out in the next tanker."

"Oh, yes," said Hyrst. "There would be several ways. I can think of a couple myself, and I've never even see the layout. The repair-lift shaft, I know, goes clear down to the feeder mechanism, and there's some kind of a system of dispersal tunnels and an emergency gadget that trips automatically to release a liquid-graphite damping material into them in case the radiation level gets too high. I don't remember that it ever did, but it's a safeguard. There'd be plenty of places to hide a lead box full of Titanite."

"Unless I show them how," repeated Shearing slowly, and began to undo the straps that held Hyrst to the table. "It has an ominous sound. I'll bet you that locating the Titanite will be child's play compared to getting it out. Well, we'll do what we can."

"The first thing," said Christina grimly, "is to get rid of Bellaver. If he has the slightest suspicion where we're headed he'll radio ahead and have all Titan alerted."

Hyrst, sitting up now on the edge of the table, hanging on against the lurching of the ship, said, "That's right — he owns the refinery now, doesn't he? Is it still working?"

"No. The mines around there played out, oh, ten, fifteen years ago. The activity's shifted to the north and east on the other side of the range. That is what may possibly give us a chance." Shearing staggered with Hyrst across the bucking deck and sat tailor-fashion in the bunk, his eyes intent. "Hyrst, I want you to remember everything you can about the refinery. The ground plan, exactly where the buildings are, the hoists, the landing field. Everything."

Hyrst said, showing the edges of his teeth, "When do I get Vernon?"

"You'll get him. I promise you."

"What about Bellaver? He's still behind us."

Shearing smiled. "That's Christina's job! Let her worry."

Hyrst nodded. He began to remember the refinery. Christina and the other two went out.

A short while later a number of things happened, violently, and in quick succession. The ship of the Lazarites, pursuing its wild and headlong course through the swarming debris of the Belt, was far ahead of Bellaver's yacht but still within instrument range. Apparently in desperation it plunged suddenly on a tangential course into a cluster of great jagged rocks all traveling together at a furious rate of speed. The cluster was perhaps two hundred miles across. The Lazarite ship twisted and turned, and then there was a swift bright flowering of flame, and then nothing.

"She's blown her tubes," said Bellaver exultantly, on the bridge of his yacht. The instruments had lost contact, chiefly because the cluster was so thick that it was impossible to separate one body from another.

Vernon said, "They're not blanking my mind anymore. It stopped, like that."

But he was still doubtful.

"Can you locate the ship?" asked Bellaver.

"I'm trying."

Bellaver caught his arm. "Look there!"

There was a second, larger and more brilliant, flash of flame.

"They've hit an asteroid," he said. "They're done for."

"I can't locate them," Vernon said. "No ship, no wreckage. It could be a trick. They could be holding a cloak."

"A trick?" said Bellaver. "I doubt it. Anyway, we're running low on fuel, and I'm not going to go into that cluster and risk my own neck to find out. If by any chance they do come out again later on, we'll deal with them."

But they both watched the cluster until it had whirled on out of sight. And neither eye nor instrument nor Vernon's probing mind could distinguish any sign of life.

VIII

*T*itan lay below them in the Saturn-glow, under the fantastic glory of the Rings. A bitter, repellent world of jagged peaks and glimmering plains of poison snow. The tiny life-raft dropped toward it, skittering nervously as it hit the thin atmosphere. Hyrst clung hard to the handholds, trying not to retch. He was not habituated to space anyway, and the skiff had been bad enough. Now, without any hull around him and nothing but a curved shield in front of him, he felt like an ant on a flying leaf.

"I don't like it either." Shearing said. "But it gives us a fifty-fifty chance of getting through unnoticed. Radar usually isn't looking for anything so small."

"*I* understand all the reasons," Hyrst said. "It's my stomach that's obtuse."

He could make out the pattern of the refinery now, a million miles of vertigo below him. The Lazarite ship was somewhere up and out behind them, hiding in the Rings. The trick had worked with Bellaver out there in the Belt, and they hoped now that it would work with Bellaver's observers on Titan. There was no need for any fake explosions this time, to give the impression of destruction. Secrecy was the watch-word, all lights out and jet-blasts muffled to a spark. Later, when Hyrst and Shearing had accomplished their mission, the ship would drop down fast and take them off, with the Titanite, before any patrol craft would have time to arrive.

They hoped.

The buildings of the refinery were dark and cold, drifted out of shape by an accumulation of the thin, evil snow. The spiderweb of roads had faded from the plain, and the landing field was smooth and un-marked. Around its perimeter the six stiff towers of the hoists stood up like lonely sentinels, hooded and cloaked.

Hyrst felt a sudden tightening of his throat, and this was a thing he had not expected. A refinery on Titan was hardly a thing to be sentimental about. But it was bound up so intimately with other things, with hopes for a future that was now far behind him, with plans for Elena and the kids that were now a cruel mockery, with friendly memories of Saul and Landers, now long dead, that he could not look at it unmoved.

"Let's try again," said Shearing quietly. "If we could locate the Titanite definitely it might make all the difference. We'll hardly have time to search all six of the bins."

Glad of the distraction, Hyrst tried. He linked his mind to Shearing's and they probed with this double probe, one after the other, the six hoists and the bins beneath them, while the raft fell whistling down the air.

It was the same as all the tries before. The bins had been empty for more than a decade, but the residual radiation was still hot enough to present a luminous haze to the eyes of the mind, fogging everything around it.

"Wait a minute," Hyrst said. "Let's use our wits. Look at the way those hoists are placed, in a wide crescent. Now if I was MacDonald, coming in from the mountains with a load of Titanite, and I wanted not to be seen, which one would I pick?"

"Either One or Six," said Shearing, without hesitation. "They're the farthest away from the buildings."

"But Number Six is at the west end of the crescent, and to reach it you would have to go clear across the landing field." He pointed mentally to Number One. "I'll bet on that one. Shall we give it another try?"

They did. This time, for a fleeting second, Hyrst thought he had something.

"So did I," said Shearing. "Sort of down under and *behind.*"

"Yes," said Hyrst. "*Look* out!" His involuntary cry was caused by the sudden collision of the life-raft with a cloud. The vapor was very thick, and after the cruel clarity of space it made Hyrst feel that he was smothering. Shearing jockeyed the raft's meager controls, and in a minute or two they were below the cloud and spiralling down toward the landing field. It was snowing.

"Good," said Shearing. "We'll hope it keeps up."

*T*hey landed close to Number One Hoist and floundered rapidly through the shallow drifts, carrying some things. The hatch had been sealed with a plastic spray to prevent corrosion, and it took them several minutes to get it open. Inside the tower it was pitch black, but they did not need lights. Their other senses showed them the worn metal treads of the steps quite clearly. In the upper chamber the indicator panels were dark and dead. Hyrst shivered inside his suit. He had been here so many times before, so long ago.

"Let's get busy," Shearing said.

They pulled on the rayproofs they had brought with them from the raft. Without power the lift was useless, but the skeleton cage, stripped of all its tools, was not too heavy for two strong men to swing clear of the shaft top. They made sure it would stay clear, and then sent down a light collapsible ladder. Hyrst slid down first into the smooth, round, totally unlighted hole, that had one segment of it open paralleling the machinery of the hoist.

"Take it carefully," Shearing said, and slid after him.

Clumsy in vac-suit and rayproof, Hyrst descended the ladder with agonizing slowness. Every impulse cried out for haste, but he knew if he hurried he would wind up at the bottom of the shaft as dead as MacDonald. The banging and knocking of their passage against the metal wall made a somber, hollow booming in that enclosed space, and it seemed to Hyrst that the silent belts and cables of the hoist hummed a little in sympathy. It was probably only the blood humming in his own ears.

"See anything yet?"

"No."

The vast strange glowing of the bin grew brighter as they approached it. The hoist was still "hot," and it glowed too, but nothing like the concentration in the bin.

"Even with rayproofs, we can't stay close to that too long."

"I don't think we'll have to. MacDonald was only human, and the bin was full then. He couldn't have stayed long either."

"See anything yet?"

"Nothing but fog. When you hit bottom, better use your light."

At long last Hyrst felt the bottom of the shaft under his boots. He stood aside from the ladder and switched on his belt lamp. In this case the physical eyes were better than the mental, being insensitive to radiation. Instantly the gears and cams of the feeder assembly sprang into sharp relief on the open side of the shaft. Shearing stumbled down off the ladder and switched on his own light.

"Where was it we thought we saw something?"

"Down under and behind." Hyrst turned slowly around, questing. The shaft was unbroken except by the repair opening. He climbed through it, with some difficulty, because nobody was supposed to climb through it and the machinery was placed for easy access with extension tools from the lift. The bin itself was now directly opposite them, a big hopper cut deep in the solid rock and serving the feeder by simple gravity. The feeder pretty well filled its own rocky chamber. A place might have been found beside it for something not too big, but the first man who came down on the lift would have seen it whether he was looking for it or not.

Shearing pointed. A dark opening pierced the rock at one side. Hyrst tried to see into it with his mental eyes, but the "fog" was so dense and bright —

He saw it, an unsubstantial ghostly shadow, but there. A square box some twenty feet down the tunnel.

Shearing drew a quick sharp breath "Let's go."

They went into the tunnel, crouching, scraping against the narrow sides.

"Look out for booby traps."

"I don't see any — yet."

The box sat in the middle of the tunnel. There was no way to get around it, no way to see over it without lying on its top and wriggling between it and the low roof. Hyrst and Shearing shut their eyes.

"I'm not sure, but I think I see a wire. Damn the fog. Can't tell where it goes —"

*H*yrst took cutters from his belt and slithered cautiously over the box. His heart was hammering very hard and his hand shook so that he had great difficulty getting the cutters and the wire together. The wire was attached to the back of the box, very crudely and hastily attached with a blob of plastic solder. It was not until he had pinched the wire with the sharp metal cutter-teeth that he realized the plastic was non-metallic and the wire bare. And then, of course, it was too late.

There must have been a simple energizer somewhere up ahead, still charging itself from the ample radiation source. The cutters flew out of Hyrst's hand in a shower of sparks, and in the darkness of the tunnel ahead there was a sudden wild flare of light, and an explosion of dust. A shock wave, not too great, hammered past Hyrst's helmet. Shearing yelled once, a protest broken short in mid-cry. Then they waited.

The dust settled. The brief tremor of the rock was stilled.

In the roof of the tunnel, where the blast had been, a broken dump-trap hung open, but nothing poured out of it but a handful of black dust.

Hyrst began to laugh. He lay on his belly on top of the box of Titanite and laughed. The tears ran out of his eyes and down his nose and dropped onto the inside of his helmet. Shearing hit him from behind. He hit him until he stopped laughing, and then Hyrst shook his head and said.

"Poor MacDonald."

"Yeah. Go ahead, you can cut the wire now."

"Such a lovely booby trap. But he wasn't figuring on time. They went away from here, Shearing, you see? And when they went they drained off the liquid graphite and took it with them. So there isn't anything left to flood the tunnel. Pathetic, isn't it?"

Shearing hit him again. "Cut the wire."

He cut it. They scuffled backward down the tunnel, dragging the box. When they got back into the shaft where there was room to do it they opened up the box.

"Doesn't look like much, does it, for all the trouble it's made?"

"No, it doesn't. But then gold doesn't look like much, or uranium, or a handful of little dry seeds." Shearing picked up a chunk of the rough, greyish ore. "You know what that is, Hyrst? That's the stars."

It was Hyrst's turn to prod Shearing into quiet. The starship and the dream that went with it were still only an intellectual interest to him. They shared out the Titanite into two webbing sacks. It made a light load for each, hardly noticeable when clipped to a belt-ring at the back.

Hyrst felt suddenly very nervous. Perhaps it was reaction, perhaps it was the memory of having been trapped in a similar hole on the Valhalla asteroid. Perhaps it was a mental premonition, obscured by the radioactive "fog." At any rate, he started to climb the ladder with almost suicidal haste, urging Shearing on after him. The shaft seemed to be a mile high. It seemed to lengthen ahead of him as he climbed, so that he was never any nearer the top. He knew it was only imagination, because he passed the level markers, but it was the closest thing to a nightmare he had ever experienced when he was broad awake. Just after they had passed the E Level mark, Shearing spoke.

"A ship has landed."

Hyrst looked mentally. The fog-effect was not so great now, and he could see quite clearly. It was a small ship, and two men were getting out of it. It had stopped snowing.

"Radar must have picked up the raft after all," said Shearing. "Or else somebody spotted the jet-flares." He began to climb faster. "We better get out of this before they come in."

D Level. Hyrst's hands were cold and stiff inside his gauntlets, clumsy hooks to catch the slender rungs. The two men were standing outside in the snow, peering around.

C Level. One of the two men saw the raft parked by the hoist tower. He pointed, and they moved toward it.

B Level. Hyrst's boots slipped and scrambled, banging the shaft wall. "Christ," said Shearing. "You sound like a temple gong. What are you trying to do, alarm the whole moon?"

*T*he men outside bent over the raft. They looked at it. Then they looked at the hoist tower. They left the raft and began to run, pulling guns out of their belts.

A Level. Hyrst's breath roared in his helmet like a great wind. He thought of the long dark way down that was below them, and how MacDonald had looked at the bottom of the shaft, and how he would take Shearing with him if he fell, and nobody would get to the stars, and Vernon would go free. He set his teeth, and sobbed, and climbed. Outside, the two men cautiously removed the hatch and stepped into the tower.

End of the ladder. A level floor to sprawl on. Hyrst squirmed away from the shaft. He thought for a minute he was going to pass out, and he fumbled with the oxygen valve, making the mixture richer. His head began to clear. Shearing was now beside him. This time they had guns, too. Shearing gave him a quick mental caution, *Not unless you have to.* One of the two men was placing a tentative foot on the stair that led up to where they were. The other man was close behind him. Shearing took careful aim and fired, at half power.

The harsh blue bolt did not strike either man. But they went reeling back in a cloud of burning flakes, and when Shearing shouted to them to drop their weapons and get out they did so, half stunned from the shock. Hyrst and Shearing leaped down the stairs, stopping only long enough to pick up the guns. Then they scrambled outside. The two men were running as hard as they could for their ship, but they had not gone far and Shearing stopped them with another shot that sent a geyser of methane steam puffing up practically under their feet.

"Not yet," he said. "Later."

The two men stood, sullenly obedient. They were both young, and not bad looking. Just doing a job, Hyrst thought. No real harm in them, just doing a job, like so many people who never stop to worry about what the job means. They both wore Bellaver's insigne on their vac-suits.

One of them said, as though he were reciting a lesson in which he had no real personal interest, "You're trespassing on private property. You'll be prosecuted to the fullest extent of the law."

"Sure," said Shearing. He motioned to the hoist tower. "Back inside."

The young men hesitated. "What you going to do?"

"Nothing fatal. It shouldn't take you more than half an hour to break out again."

He marched them to the hatch and saw them inside it. Hyrst was watching the sky, the black star-glittering sky with the glorious arch of the Rings across it and one milky-bright curve of Saturn visible and growing above the eastern horizon.

"They're coming," he said mentally to Shearing.

"Good." He started to close the hatch, and one of the young men pointed suddenly to the sack clipped to Shearing's belt.

"You've been stealing something."

"Tell that to Bellaver."

"You bet I will. The fullest extent of the law, mister! The fullest extent —"

The hatch closed. Shearing jammed the fastening mechanism so it could not be turned from the inside. Then he went and stood beside Hyrst in the glimmering plain, watching the ship drop down out of the Rings.

Hyrst said, "They'll tell Bellaver."

"Naturally."

"What will Bellaver do?"

"I'm not sure. Something drastic. He wants our starship so hard he'd murder his own children to get it. You can see why. In itself it's priceless, a hundred years ahead of its time, but that's not all. It's what it stands for. To us it means freedom and safety. To Bellaver it means —"

He gestured toward the sky, and Hyrst nodded, seeing in Shearing's mind the image of a gigantic Bellaver, ten times bigger than God, gathering the whole galaxy into his arms.

"I wish you luck," said Hyrst. He unhooked the sack of Titanite from his belt and gave it to Shearing. "It'll take a little while to refine the stuff and build the relays, even so. That may be time enough. Come back for me if you can."

"Vernon?"

"Yes."

Shearing nodded. "I said I'd help you get him. I will."

"No. This is my job. I'll do it alone. You belong there, with them. With Christina."

"Hyrst. Listen —"

"Don't tell me where the starship is. I might not hold out as well as you."

"All right, but Hyrst — in case we can't get back — look for us away from the Sun. Not toward it."

"I'll remember."

The ship landed. Shearing entered it, carrying the Titanite. And Hyrst walked away, toward the closed and buried buildings of the refinery.

It had begun to snow again.

IX

*I*t was cold and dark and infinitely sad. Hyrst wandered through the rooms, feeling like a ghost, thinking like one. Everything had been removed from the buildings. The living quarters were now mere cubicular tombs for a lot of memories, absolutely bare of any human or familiar touch. It felt very strange to Hyrst. He kept telling himself that fifty years had passed, but he could not believe it. It seemed only a few months since MacDonald's death, months occupied by investigation and trial and the raging, futile anguish of the unjustly accused. The long interval of the pseudo-death was no more than a night's sleep, to a mind unconscious of passing time. Now it seemed that Saul and Landers should still be here, and there should be lights and warmth and movement.

There was nothing. He could not bring himself to stay in the living quarters. He went into one of the storerooms and sat on a concrete buttress and waited. It was a long and dreadful wait. During it all the emotional storms occasioned by the murder and its aftermath passed through his mind. Scenes with Saul and Landers. Scenes with the investigators, with Mac-

Donald's family, with lawyers and reporters. Scenes with Elena. The whole terrible nightmare, leading inevitably to that culminating moment when the door of the airlock opened and he joined the sleepers on the plain. When it was all over Hyrst felt shaken and exhausted, but calm. The face of Vernon burned brightly in his mind's eye.

Without bothering to open the steel-shuttered windows, he watched the two young men force their way out of the hoist tower. He watched them run to their ship and chatter excitedly over their radio. By the time, much later, that Bellaver's yacht came screaming down to the landing field on a flaming burst of jets, he could watch it with almost the cool detachment of a spectator. He was careful to keep his shields up tight against Vernon, and he did not think the other Lazarite would be likely to look for him. Vernon seemed to be fully occupied with Bellaver.

"What else would they be stealing, you fool? You should have killed Hyrst before, when you had the chance."

"Somebody had to take the blame for MacDonald. Anyway, you had him aboard the Happy Dream. *Why didn't you hang onto him?"*

"Don't get insolent with me, Vernon. I can turn you over to the police anytime, for any one of a hundred things."

"Not without tipping your hand, Bellaver."

"It would be worth it." A string of foul names, delivered in a furious scream. *"You couldn't locate the Titanite, but they did, just as soon as they got hold of Hyrst."*

"All right, Mr. God Almighty Bellaver, turn me in. But if it was the Titanite they took, you haven't a chance of finding that starship without me."

"You haven't done very well at it so far."

"In the excitement, they may get careless. But it's up to you."

More foul language, but Bellaver did not repeat his threat. He and Vernon, with a couple of other men, got into vac-suits and lumbered across the snow to the hoist tower. From inside the cold dark buried building, Hyrst watched them, and thought hard and fast, and smiled. Presently he left the building and circled cautiously through the snowy gloom until he was in range of their helmet-communicators. He could hear them aurally now, but he kept watching them, esper-fashion.

*T*hey inspected the empty lead box, and the young men told what had happened, and Bellaver turned his raging fury against them. There was no longer any doubt that the Titanite had been found and taken away, and Bellaver saw the stars and worlds and moons, the bright glowing plunder of a galaxy, slipping away from him. He threatened the two young men with every punishment he could think of for not having stopped the thieves, and one of the young men turned white and anxious, and the other one flushed brick red and shook his fist close to Bellaver's helmet.

"You go to hell," he said. "I don't care who you are. You go to hell."

He walked out of the hoist tower, with his companion stumbling at his heels, and Bellaver screamed after them, and behind him the crewmen looked shocked and contemptuous, and Vernon laughed openly, showing the edges of his teeth.

The two young men got into their ship and went away. Bellaver turned and stood looking at the empty box. He seemed exhausted now, hopeless, like a child about to break down and cry. Vernon went over and kicked the box.

"Hyrst had the advantage," he said. "He knew Mac-Donald and he knew the refinery. Even so, it must have been pure guesswork. Nobody could probe through that fog."

"What are we going to do?" asked Bellaver. "Vernon, what are we going to do?"

Hyrst spoke for the first time, his voice ringing loud and startling in their ears.

"Don't ask Vernon," he said. "Ask me."

There was a moment of complete silence. Hyrst felt Vernon's mind brush his, and he permitted himself one cruel flash of triumph. Then everybody spoke at once, Vernon explaining why he hadn't spotted Hyrst — who could have figured he'd stay behind at a time like this? — the crew-members nervously fingering their guns, and Bellaver crying,

"Hyrst! Is that you, Hyrst? Where are you?"

"Where I can get the first shot at anybody coming out of the tower, and where nobody from the yacht will ever reach me. Tell them all to stay put. Go ahead, Bellaver, you want to hear me out, don't you?"

"What do you want to say?"

"I can find you that starship. Tell them, Bellaver."

He told them. And Vernon said to Bellaver, "If he's willing to betray his friends, why would he get them the Titanite?" He laughed. "It isn't even a good trick."

"Oh, yes, it is," said Hyrst softly. "It's a very good one. The best. You see, I don't care about the starship or the Titanite. All I care about is the man who killed MacDonald. They were sort of bound up together. Ever hear of latent impressions, Vernon? I was unconscious, but my ears heard and my eyes saw, and my brain remembered, when it was shown how."

"That was fifty years ago," said Vernon. "People don't understand about us. Nobody would believe you if you told them."

"They would if Bellaver told them. They would if Bellaver explained out loud about the Lazarites, about what happens to men when they go through the door. They'd listen to him. And there must be others who know, or at least suspect." Hyrst paused, long enough to smile. "The beauty of that is, Bellaver, that you're in the clear. You're not responsible for a murder your grandfather had done. You could swear you didn't even know about it until now."

Vernon said to Bellaver, "If you do this to me, I'll blast you wide open."

"What can he do, Bellaver?" Hyrst shouted. "He can talk, but you have the money, the position, the legal powers. You can talk louder. And when they know the truth, will anybody take the word of a Lazarite against a human man?"

His voice rose higher and louder, drowning out Vernon's cry.

"Are you afraid of him, Bellaver? Are you so afraid of him you'll let the starship go?"

"Hold him." Bellaver said, and the crewmen held Vernon fast. "Wait a minute, Hyrst," he said. "What's your angle? Is it just revenge? Are you selling out your friends for something over and done half a century ago? I don't believe it, Hyrst."

Hyrst said slowly, "I can answer that, so even you will understand. I have children. They're getting old now. They've lived all their lives thinking their father killed a man, not for love or for justice or in self-defense, but for sheer cold-blooded greed. I want them to know it wasn't so."

"Hold him!" Bellaver said. The crewmen struggled with Vernon, and Vernon said viciously to Bellaver,

"He'll never lead you to the starship. I can read his mind. When you've turned me in and blackened your grandfather's name to clear him, he'll laugh in your face. What are you, Bellaver, a fool?"

"Am I, Hyrst?"

"That's for you to find out. I'm offering you the starship for Vernon, and that's fair enough, because I want him as bad as you want it. And I can tell you, Bellaver, if you decide to play it smart and call in your guards to hunt me down, it will do you no good. I won't be alive when they take me."

Silence. In his mind's eye Hyrst could see the beads of sweat running down Bellaver's face behind his helmet. He could see Vernon's face, too. It gave him pleasure.

"It should be an easy decision, Bellaver," he said. "After all, suppose I am lying. What have you got to lose but Vernon? And with his record, that isn't much."

"Hold him," said Bellaver. "All right, Hyrst. I'll do it. But I'll tell you now. If you lie to me, there won't be any re-awakening in another fifty years. This will be for good."

"Fair enough," said Hyrst. "I'm putting my gun away. I'm coming in."

He walked quickly through the snow toward the tower.

X

On the bridge of his yacht, Bellaver turned to Hyrst and said,

"I've done what you wanted. Now find me that starship."

Hyrst nodded. "Take off."

The rockets roared and thundered, and the swift yacht leaped quivering into the sky.

Hyrst sat quietly in his recoil chair. He felt a different man, changed entirely in the last few days. Much had happened in those days.

Bellaver had got busy on the radio even before his yacht left Titan, and the story of the Lazarites had burst like a nova upon the Solar System. Already there were instances of suspected Lazarites being mobbed by their neighbors, and Government was frantically concerning itself with all the new, far-reaching implications of the Humane Penalty.

Close on the heels of this bomb-shell had come Vernon's angry accusations against Bellaver, delivered as soon as he was given to the authorities on Mars. During the twenty Martian hours necessary for formal charge and the taking of depositions, and while Bellaver's yacht was being refueled, Vernon's story of the starship went out on all the interworld circuits. And it had been as Christina had said. The whole Solar System was frantic to have the Lazarites caught and stopped, and every man in space became a self-appointed searcher for the hidden starship. Bellaver, letting his lawyers worry about Vernon's accusations, had already laid formal claim to that ship, based on the value of the stolen Titanite.

"Where?" demanded Bellaver now, in a fury of impatience. "Where?"

"Wait," said Hyrst. "There are too many watching, ready to follow you. They know what you're after. Wait till we're clear of Mars."

He sat in his chair, looking into space. His drive was all gone, and the anger that had fed it. Somewhere his son and his two daughters were drawing their first free breaths relieved of a burden they should never have had to carry. They knew now that he was innocent, and they could think of him now without bitterness, speak his name without hate. He had done what he had set out to do, and he was finished. He knew what was ahead of him, but he was too tired to care.

The yacht went fast, away from the old red weary planet. Hyrst thought of Shearing and Christina and the others, laboring over their ship on the dark plain. He felt safe in doing this, because Vernon was gone and the grey evil man who had helped to torture Shearing aboard the *Happy Dream* was still in an Earth hospital recovering from the blow Hyrst had given him. They were out of reach, and Hyrst was the only Lazarite Bellaver had.

He did not try to get through to Shearing because he knew that was impossible, and there was no reason for it anyway. He let his mind stretch out and rove through the nighted spaces beyond Saturn, beyond

Uranus and Neptune, beyond the black and frigid bulk of Pluto. He did not see the ship nor touch a Lazarite mind, and so he knew that they were still holding the cloak, still hiding from possible betrayal. He withdrew his mind, and wished them luck.

"We're clear of Mars," said Bellaver. "Which way?"

"That way," said Hyrst, and pointed. "Toward the Sun."

The yacht swerved and steadied on a new course, toward the distant glare of Sol. And Bellaver said,

"What's the exact location?"

"Can you trust every man in this crew?" asked Hyrst. "Can you be sure not one of them would give it away, when we stop to refuel? You're not the only one that knows about the starship now, remember."

"You could tell *me.*"

"You're too impatient, Bellaver. You'd want to head straight there, and it won't be that easy. They have defenses. We have to be careful, or they'll destroy the ship before we reach it."

"Or finish their relays and go." Bellaver gave Hyrst a long look. "I'll trust you because I have to. But I wasn't making an empty threat. And I'll do it so there won't be any thought of murder. You'd better find me that ship, Hyrst."

From then on, Bellaver hardly slept. He paced the corridors and haunted the control room and watched Hyrst with a gnawing, agonizing doubt. Hyrst began to feel for him a distant sort of pity, as he might have felt for a man afflicted by some disease brought on by his own excesses.

*T*he yacht passed the orbit of Earth, refueled at an obscure space station, and sped on. Hyrst continued to stall Bellaver, ordering a change of course from time to time to keep him happy. At intervals he let his mind rove through those dark spaces they were leaving farther behind with every passing second. Each time it was a greater effort, but still there was no sign of the starship or its base, and so he knew that the labor still went on.

By the time the yacht reached the orbit of Venus a fan-shaped cordon of other ships had collected around and behind her drawn by the word that Bellaver was on his way to find the starship. Government patrols were in constant touch.

"They can't interfere," said Bellaver. "I've got a lien on that ship, a formal claim."

"Sure," said Hyrst. "But you'd better be the first to find it. Possession, you know. Bear off a bit. Mislead them. They're sure now they know where you're going."

"Don't they?" said Bellaver, looking ahead at the glittering spark that was Mercury. "There isn't anyplace else to go."

"Isn't there?"

Bellaver stared at him, narrow-eyed. "The legend of the Vulcan was exploded by the first explorers. There is no intra-Mercurial world."

Hyrst shot a swift stabbing mental glance toward Pluto. Still nothing. He sighed and said easily,

"There wasn't then. There is now."

He brazened out the look of incredulity on Bellaver's face.

"These are Lazarites, remember, not men. They built a place for themselves where nobody would ever think to look. Not a planet, of course, just a floating workshop. A satellite. And now you know. So you can let them beat you to Mercury."

"All right," said Bellaver softly. "All right."

They passed Mercury, lost in the blaze of the Sun, and only a few ships followed them, far behind. The rest stopped to search the craggy valleys of the Twilight Belt, and the bleak icefields of the Dark Side.

And now Hyrst had run his string out, and he knew it. When no intra-Mercurial satellite showed up, physically or on detector-screens, there was no further lie to tell. He drove his mind out and away, to the cold planets wheeling on the fringes of Sol's light, and he sweated, and prayed, and hoped that nothing had gone wrong. And suddenly the cloak was dropped, and he saw a lonesome chip of rock beyond Pluto, all hollowed out for shops and living quarters, and the great ship standing in the mile-long plain, with the stars all drifted overhead. And the ship lifted from the plain, circled upward, and suddenly was not.

Hyrst was bitterly sorry that he was not aboard. But he told Bellaver, "You can stop looking now. They've got away."

He watched Bellaver die, standing erect on his feet, still breathing, but dying inside with the last outgoing of hope.

"I thought you were lying," he said, "but it was the only chance I had." He nodded, looking toward the shuttered port with the insufferable blaze outside. He said, in a flat, dead voice, "If you were put out here, bound, in a lifeboat, headed toward the Sun — Yes. I could make up a story to fit that."

In the same toneless voice, he called his men. And suddenly the yacht lurched over shuddering in the backwash of some tremendous energy. Hyrst and the others were flung scattering against the bulk-heads, and the lights went out, and the instruments went dead.

Beyond the port, on the unshuttered side away from the Sun, a vast dark shape had materialized out of nothing, to hang close in space beside the yacht.

Hyrst heard in his mind, strong and clear, the voice of Shearing saying, "Didn't I tell you the brotherhood stands by its own? Besides, we couldn't make a liar out of you, now could we?"

Hyrst began to laugh, just a little bit hysterically. He told Bellaver, "There's your starship. And Shearing says if I'm not alive when he comes aboard to get me, that they won't be as careful about warping space when they go away as they were when they came."

Bellaver did not say anything. He sat on the deck where the shock had thrown him, not speaking. He was still sitting there when Hyrst passed through the airlock into the starship's boat, and he did not move even when the great ship vanished silently into whatever mysterious ultra-space the minds of the Lazarites had unlocked, outbound for the limitless freedom of the universe, where the wheeling galaxies thunder on forever across infinity and the stars burn bright, and there is nothing to stop the march of the Legion of Lazarus. And who knew, who could tell, where that march would end?

Aboard the starship, already a million miles away, Hyrst said to Christina. "When they brought me back from beyond the door, that was re-awakening. But this — this is being born again."

She did not answer that. But she took his hand and smiled.

www.ingramcontent.com/pod-product-compliance
Lightning Source LLC
Chambersburg PA
CBHW030150200626
46812CB00016B/1777